Swim, Jim!

KAZ WINDNESS

A Paula Wiseman Book
Simon & Schuster Books for Young Readers
New York London Toronto Sydney New Delhi

For Lily

SIMON & SCHUSTER BOOKS FOR YOUNG READERS
An imprint of Simon & Schuster Children's Publishing Division
1230 Avenue of the Americas, New York, New York 10020
© 2022 by Kaz Windness
Book design by Laurent Linn © 2022 by Simon & Schuster, Inc.

For information about special discounts for bulk purchases, please contact Simon & Schuster Special Sales
at 1-866-506-1949 or business@simonandschuster.com.
The Simon & Schuster Speakers Bureau can bring authors to your live event. For more information or to book an event,
contact the Simon & Schuster Speakers Bureau at 1-866-248-3049 or visit our website at www.simonspeakers.com.
The text for this book was set in Banda Regular.
The illustrations for this book were rendered using graphite on paper and painted digitally in Adobe Photoshop.
Manufactured in China
0222 SCP
First Edition
2 4 6 8 10 9 7 5 3 1
Library of Congress Cataloging-in-Publication Data
Names: Windness, Kaz, 1974- author, illustrator.
Title: Swim, Jim! / Kaz Windness.
Description: First edition. | New York : Simon & Schuster Books for Young Readers, [2022] |
Includes bibliographical references. | Audience: Ages 4–8. | Audience: Grades 2-3. |
Summary: With the help of his sisters and some borrowed floaties, a fearful crocodile learns to swim.
Includes information about crocodiles.
Identifiers: LCCN 2021016542 (print) | LCCN 2021016543 (ebook) |
ISBN 9781534483439 (hardcover) | ISBN 9781534483446 (ebook)
Subjects: CYAC: Fear—Fiction. | Swimming—Fiction. |
Brothers and sisters—Fiction. | Crocodiles—Fiction.
Classification: LCC PZ7.1.W5837 Sw 2022 (print) | LCC PZ7.1.W5837 (ebook) | DDC [E]—dc23
LC record available at https://lccn.loc.gov/2021016542
LC ebook record available at https://lccn.loc.gov/2021016543

On a moonlit night in Swigwater Swamp,
out hatched three baby crocodiles.

Jim's toe.

"Swim, Jim!" called Sim.
"Um . . . maybe later," said Jim.
"HA-HA!" laughed Kim. "Jim can't swim!"

Jim peered down into the deep, dark water.
"Are you afraid of swimming?" asked Ma.
"No," said Jim. "I'm afraid of sinking."

"More like *stinking*!" teased Kim.

"SINKING! STINKING! JIM CAN'T SWIM!" said Sim.

"Don't worry, Jim.
You'll swim when you're ready,"
said Pa.

But Jim was already hatching a plan
to prove his sisters wrong.

Early next morning,
Jim wiggle-waggled
out of Swigwater Swamp.

Dear Family,
Our swamp is too deep,
too dark, and too BIG.
I'm off to find a
little swamp.
Then I'll show you,
Jim Can Swim!

Jim wiggled far . . .

he waggled wide . . .

But he couldn't find a little swamp anywhere.
"Now I'll never learn to swim!" cried Jim.

Just then,
Jim heard a
SPLISH!

Then he heard a
SPLASH!

Could it be?

"Only if you trade me your noodle."

The floaties and noodles kept the strange crocodiles from sinking.
I've got to try those! thought Jim.

How nice of them to leave their things for me, thought Jim.

CAKE!

"Jim must be around here somewhere," said Kim.

"What are you doing here?" asked Jim.
"Looking for you, silly!" said Kim.

"What are you wearing?" asked Sim.
"These will keep me from sinking,"
said Jim.

"Do they really work?" asked Sim.
"Only one way to find out!" said Kim.

"Here I go!" shouted Jim.

"Hey! I'm NOT sinking!"

"HELP! I'M SINKING!"

"No, we're floating!"
said Sim.

"Floating is nice,"
said Jim.

"But you could just
stand up," said Kim.

"Oh," said Jim.

"Floating is only part of swimming," said Kim. "But we can teach you!"

"Uh-oh! Time to go!"
cried Sim.

Wiggle-Waggle
Wiggle-Waggle-WHEE!

"You naughty crocs.
Let's go back home!"

"Come watch me swim!"
said Jim.

CROCODILE FACTS

Are crocodiles reptiles? Yes! Reptiles lay eggs and are cold-blooded, which means their body temperature changes based on their surroundings. For this reason, many crocodiles prefer to live in warm, tropical climates.

Do crocodiles need help staying afloat? No, crocodiles are natural-born swimmers. But Jim's story was inspired by a real-life photograph in the *Miami Herald* of a crocodile swimming in a canal with a pool noodle under its belly.

Do crocodiles swim in pools? Yes, they have been known to stop by for a dip! Crocodiles move from one body of water to another looking for new territory, mates, and food. A pool can look a lot like a little swamp to a crocodile.

Do crocodiles live in swamps? Yes! Most crocodiles live near freshwater lakes and rivers. But like Jim, some crocodiles live in brackish (a mix of saltwater and freshwater) swamps.

How can you tell the difference between crocodiles and alligators? Alligators have rounded snouts, while crocodiles have pointy ones. Crocodile smiles are toothier, too. The Florida Everglades is the only place on Earth where alligators and crocodiles coexist.

Do crocodiles stay with their mothers after they hatch? Yes! Most mother crocodiles lay their eggs on land and cover them with mud to keep them warm and safe. For up to three months, a mother crocodile waits near her nest, protecting her eggs from predators. As soon as the baby crocodiles are ready to hatch, they start to chirp. The mother digs down to the eggs and carries her newborn babies to the water in her mouth. The babies stay with her for up to two years.

Do crocodiles fart? Yes! Just like people, reptiles fart to release gas trapped inside their bellies.

BIBLIOGRAPHY

"The Difference Between the Alligators & Crocodiles of the Everglades." *Everglades Holiday Park*, evergladesholidaypark.com/difference-gators-crocodiles. Accessed March 9, 2021.

Feldman, Thea, and Lee Cosgrove. *Alligators and Crocodiles Can't Chew! (Super Facts for Super Kids)*. Illustrated, New York: Simon & Schuster, 2021.

Marr, Madeleine. "Yes, that's a crocodile on a pool noodle. No, the human didn't get it back." *Miami Herald*, 22 August, 2018, miamiherald.com/news/state/florida/article217025005.html.

"Nile Crocodile." *National Geographic Animals*, kids.nationalgeographic.com/animals/reptiles/facts/nile-crocodile. Accessed March 9, 2021.